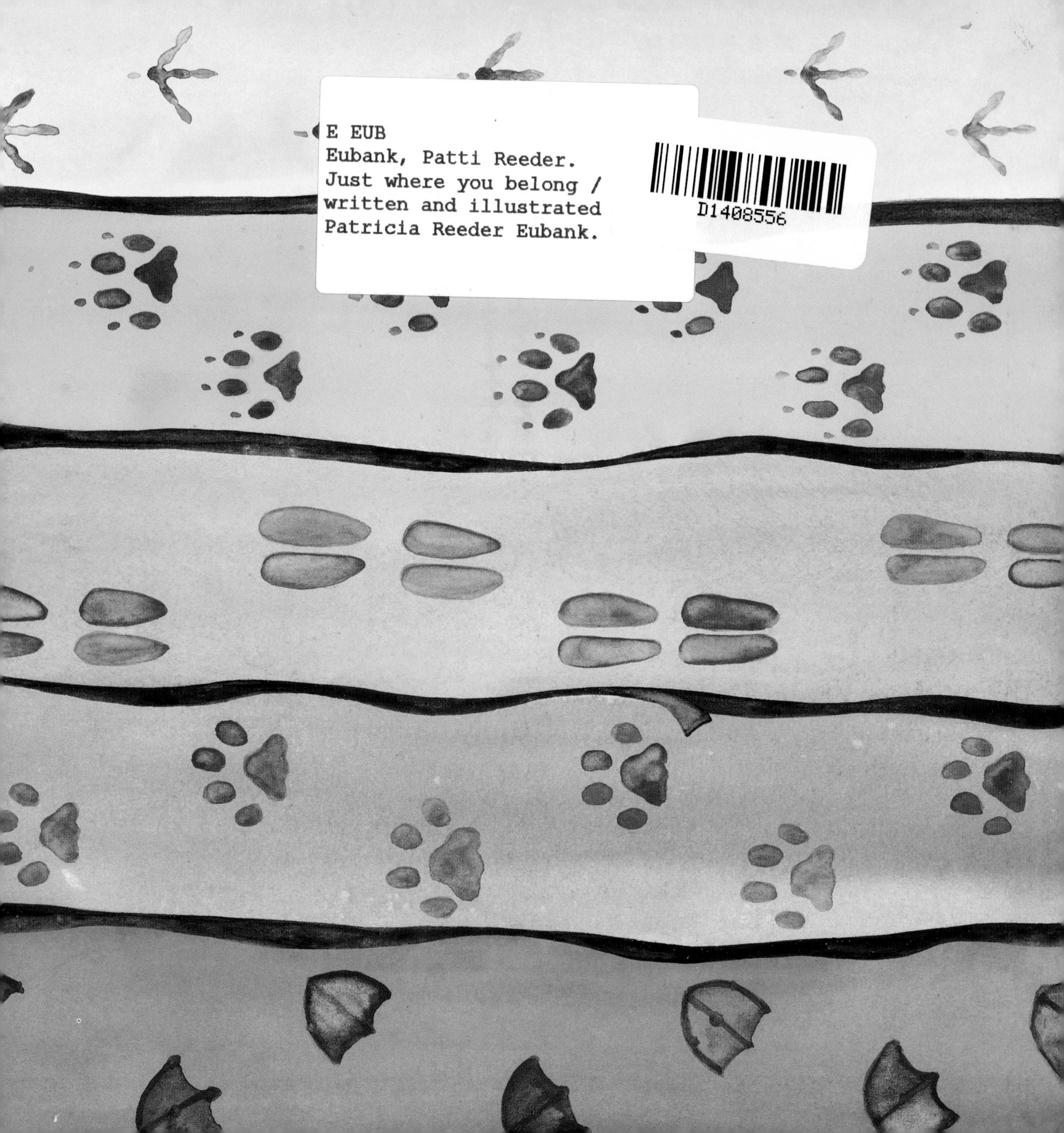

Just Where You Belong

This book belongs to

____

Just Where You Belong

Written and Illustrated by Patricia Reeder Eubank

ideals children's books™
Nashville, Tennessee

ISBN 0-8249-5481-5
Published by Ideals Children's Books
An imprint of Ideals Publications
A division of Guideposts
535 Metroplex Drive, Suite 250
Nashville, Tennessee 37211
www.idealsbooks.com

Color separations by Precision Color Graphics, Franklin, Wisconsin

Printed and bound in Italy

Library of Congress CIP data on file

Designed by Eve DeGrie

10 9 8 7 6 5 4 3 2 1

For Mom

One day Little Rhino and his friends were playing hide-and-seek.

"You're it, Little Rhino," called Little Giraffe.

Little Rhino put his head down in the soft grass and hid his eyes.

"One, two, three," counted Little Rhino. "Four, five, six," whispered Little Rhino. "Seven . . . eight . . . nine . . ." counted Little Rhino.

Little Rhino had counted himself to sleep.

When Little Rhino woke up, he looked around. "Oh, no!" he cried. "Where is everybody? Where is Little Giraffe? I've lost my mama!"

Little Rhino jumped to his feet and set out to find his mama.

Little Rhino ran over
to a gaggle of geese.
"Have you seen my
mama?" he asked.

"No, no" the geese
giggled. "But waddle
with us."

"No, thanks. I better
not straggle with
the gaggle."

"Have you seen my mama?"
he asked a covey of quail.

"Oh, no!" the quail shook
their heads. "But stay with us."

"No, thanks," said
Little Rhino. "I can't be
lovey-dovey with a covey."

Little Rhino ran up to a flock of sheep grazing on the hillside. "Have you seen my mama?" he questioned.

"Nooooo," the sheep shook their woolly heads. "Stay and meander with us."

"No, thanks, I can't climb a rock with the flock!"

Little Rhino looked up. A pride of lions lay snoozing in the tree. “Have you seen my mama?” he called.

“No!” the lions roared and twitched their tails. “But join us on a limb,” they purred.

“No, thanks,” replied Little Rhino, “I can’t hide with the pride.”

Little Rhino ran over to a herd of elephants splashing. "Have you seen my mama?" he asked.

"No! No!" they trumpeted. "But come walk with us."

"No, thanks," laughed Little Rhino.
"To walk with your herd is absurd."

Little Rhino trudged over to a pack of wolves sunning themselves by their den. “Have you seen my mama?”
“Ah, no,” they howled. “But please, rest awhile.”
“No, thanks. I can’t lay back with a pack.”

Little Rhino swam over to a pod of seals climbing on the rocks. “Have you seen my mama?” he asked.

“No, no,” the seals barked. “But stay here with us.”

“No thank you,” said Little Rhino. “I can’t trod with a pod.”

“Have you seen my mama?” Little Rhino shouted at a gam of blue whales diving in the ocean.

“We have not,” they spouted. “But come and play.”

“No, thanks,” said Little Rhino,
“I can’t say that I swam with a gam!”

A troop of kangaroos came hopping by. "Did you pass my mama back there?" called Little Rhino.

"Nope, but you can march with us!" they hollered as they bounced past him.

"No, thanks," sighed Little Rhino. "A troop is not my group."

Then, Little Rhino came to a prickle of porcupines and a conflagration of fireflies. "Excuse me, have you seen my mama?" Little Rhino asked.

"No, but you can join us."

"No, thanks," chuckled Little Rhino. "It won't tickle to be with the prickle as the conflagration changes location."

Little Rhino ambled on until, suddenly, he heard . . .

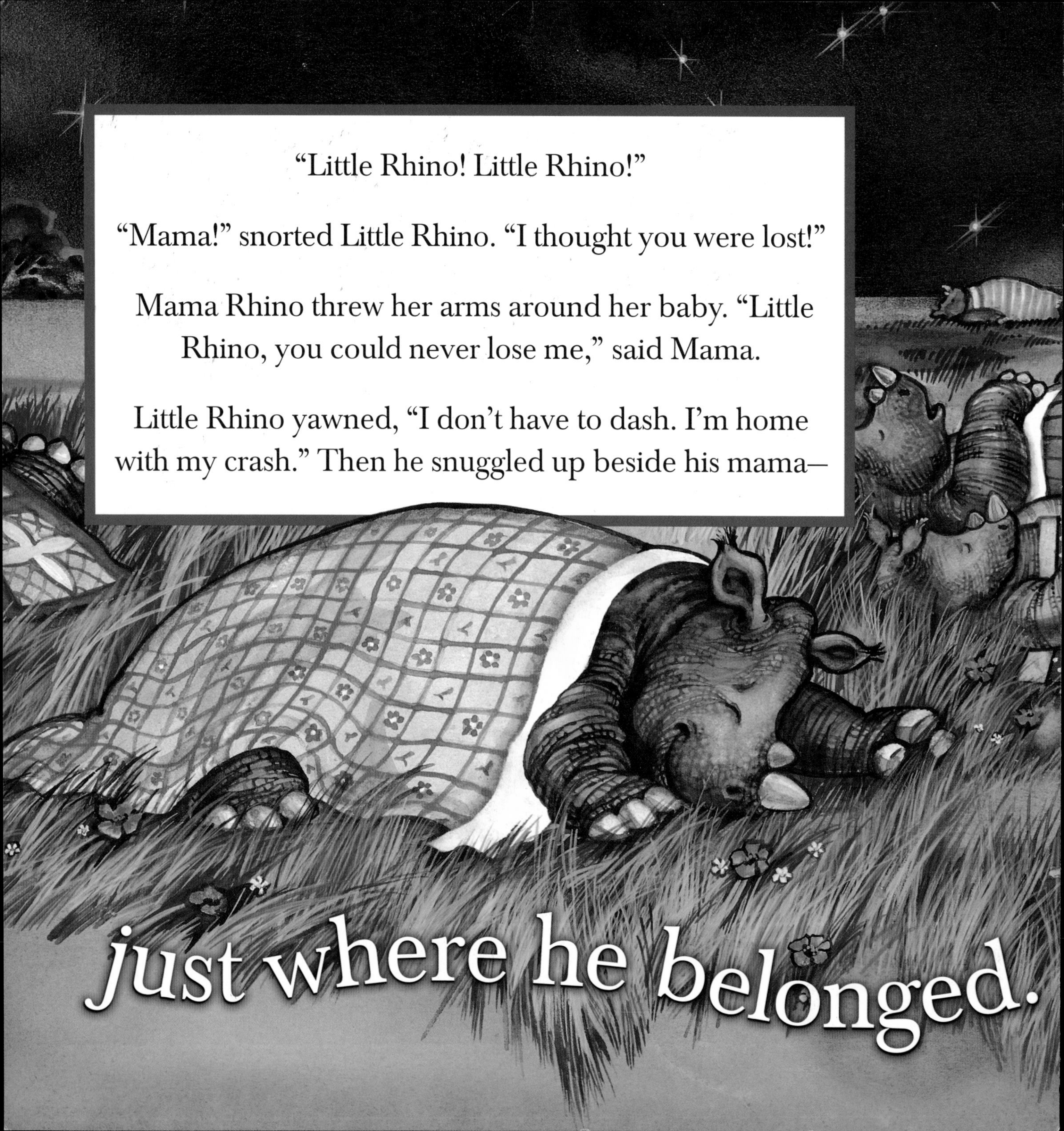
"Little Rhino! Little Rhino!"
"Mama!" snorted Little Rhino. "I thought you were lost!"
Mama Rhino threw her arms around her baby. "Little Rhino, you could never lose me," said Mama.
Little Rhino yawned, "I don't have to dash. I'm home with my crash." Then he snuggled up beside his mama–
just where he belonged.

The groups of animals that Little Rhino met—

gaggle of geese
covey of quail
flock of sheep
pride of lions
herd of elephants
pack of wolves
pod of seals
gam of whales
troop of kangaroos
prickle of porcupines
conflagration of fireflies
crash of rhinoceros